I0451534

Soulless Light

By

Joann Hamann-Buchanan

World Castle Publishing
http://www.worldcastlepublishing.com

Joann H. Buchannan

World Castle Publishing
Pensacola, Florida
Copyright © Joann Hamann-Buchanan 2011
ISBN: 9781937593551
First Edition World Castle Publishing September 15, 2011
http://www.worldcastlepublishing.com
Licensing Notes
Cover Artist: Robert Hunyor
Editor: Beth Price

Soulless Light
Haunting in my desires
Thrilled by what is flawed.
I see now that which before could not be seen.
The gray matter of us all
The soul
The light
The sparkle of the infinite night.
Seeking only to be heard
cause we are all dead or dying.
And there in lies the truth of that
which I am buying.
I'm gonna live forever
in the dark of night.
Alive but dead
Dead but alive
Does it even matter?
I'm lost now in a day dream
of my own creation.
Living
And
Dead
Am I the soulless light?

Joann H. Buchannan

The Beginning

The pestilence of death lingered throughout the lands in the year Thirteen sixty-three. The winds of the four lands carried the stench of the burned carcasses throughout, leaving no area untarnished. All innocence lay lost in a sea of superstition and hope was just the Bloodstained tip of a blade carried by the Bishops Templar Knights—a group of soldiers who fought for the Bishop, allegedly carried out God's word. In truth they were nothing more than murderous thieves whose actions were covered in a vale of darkness by the plague.

The now petrified forest is an evil reminder of pain and suffering—a ghost of a time long forgotten. It guards the remnants of a village in the middle of a lake called The Isle of Ely. Sharp reeds grow along the edges of the natural lake mote. A single path leads from the ferry towards the village. Hungry eyes rode upon horses the day death arrived.

According to Bishop William we were already guilty of conspiring with the devil. Though we knew nothing of it and considered ourselves to be blessed by God and all He had to offer in His glory. We each had a sin that stained our souls, as did all man—still not one warranted the Bloodstained earth that fell upon us.

Bishop William was a young man who had made his way through the ranks by being able to prove his accusations of devil worship and witchcraft. The simplest of accusations are often the most damming—a lesson I would soon learn the hard way.

Compared to now, I was but a child when the only place I knew became the very reminder of death. I was pure, young and in love with Joseph, son of Ruth, the village midwife. The fiery floods of passion filled our hearts with a longing like no other. We were to be married in less than a month and I couldn't keep my body from lusting for him.

Growing up as I did made it almost too easy to fall in love with Joseph. We had always been friends. My dear sweet Joseph, the man I knew as a boy, had been the love of my life-my whole life. Oh how I would have made a different choice had I only known the cost. I'm lifted into an eternal damnation of my own making.

The rising sun appeared in the sky like a dragon's eye looking down upon us— watching over us like a magical force sent from above. Perhaps it was nothing more than an observant spirit. I would believe that now. Then I took it as a blessing, a sign from above because no matter how many breaths I took around Joseph, I still couldn't breathe. We met when we were nothing more than children. I remember when I would get so angry at him for pulling my hair and running off. When one's a child, young love can show itself in the most violent of ways.

At the age of 10, I was sent to work for Ruth. I walked to her home in the early morning hours and knocked on her door — nervous knots tightened in my stomach. Ruth opened the door with a flushed look on her face. A woman yelled out in pain from beyond the bedroom door.

She looked down at me, "Just in time child, go fetch me a pale of water."

Ruth handed me a bucket and shut the door. 'Does water ease a woman's pain in childbirth?' I didn't know. I felt the urgency in her request and away I went. I walked down to the well and brought it back as quickly as my little legs could carry me.

Timid—I opened the door to her home and walked in with the bucket. She yelled out from behind the door.

"Put some water on the stove to boil," she said.

In the back ground, I heard a woman, who I would later know as Rebecca, crying out in pain. A knock sounded on the door. I opened it to find a nervous man named Peter.

"I heard my wife was here, giving birth. Is she ok?" Peter asked.

I jumped at the scream from the other room. I turned back to look at the closed door then looked back at the man. He rocked from side to side with a nervous painful look on his face.

"She's here," I said, voice calm but unsteady.

Relief rushed through me when Joseph appeared from out of nowhere. I didn't know he was in the stables in the back tending to the horses.

"Why is this happening here?" Peter asked.

"I do not know, I just arrived and fetched some water," I told him.

"You're Julia, right?" Joseph asked.

"I am," I said.

"I'm Joseph, Ruth's son."

"She went to market earlier," Peter interrupted.

"Then our house must have been the closest," Joseph said. "Not to worry, my mom knows what she's doing. You better stay out here. I'll keep you company."

With that, Joseph reached past me and closed the door. I was left inside the house with little idea as to what I was supposed to do. When the water reached boiling, I knocked on the door to the bedroom. Ruth opened the door and grabbed my hand.

"Go by her head and help hold her legs. We're going to birth a child right now," she said.

Awkward, unsteady, I followed Ruth's instructions and pressed one of Rebecca's legs towards her head. Rebecca let out a grunt and some deep breaths. Her face, covered with sweat and flushed, scrunched up into almost nothing.

"That's right, Rebecca, almost there. Keep pushing the little thing out," she said.

Breath didn't reach my lungs while I held her leg. She took my hand and squeezed so hard I thought I would pass out from the pain. I didn't utter a word in defense. Ruth looked up at me with a slight grin on her face.

"You're about to witness the most precious miracle God gave us. Come on, Rebecca, one more time," she said.

Rebecca bore down again. This time, a tiny blue creature rushed out of her. It was covered in a red and brown goo. Ruth cleaned the baby up and smacked it on the behind showing the small protrusion dangling between his legs.

"A fine healthy boy for your husband," Ruth said.

The newborn's scream sent a wave of love through the room. Rebecca, visibly exhausted, couldn't wait to hold her son. He took right away to suckling on her breast.

"Remember the water?" she said to me.

I nodded my head.

"Good, go put a rag in it and wring it out so I can clean her and the baby up," she told me.

I walked out to the stove, took a couple rags, dipped them in the water, wrung them out and took them to Ruth. She waved them in the air to cool them off and began to wipe away the blood and fluids from Rebecca. A few seconds later, Joseph knocked on the door.

"Peter's here," he said.

"I'll be out in a minute," Ruth said.

"Too late, he's outside the door," he said.

Ruth left the three of us in the room. I watched Rebecca smile down at the little boy with a joy I had only seen from a distance.

"Are they both — ?"

"They are," Ruth said. "You have a son. A fine healthy boy."

"A son! Praise God!" Excitement filled his voice.

"You can come in just as soon as she's all cleaned," Ruth said. "Joseph, give Peter some hospitality while I finish with Rebecca."

We finished cleaning Rebecca up. She passed out from the strenuous ordeal with the tiny baby boy in her arms. A few minutes later, the two of us walked out of the room and Peter was allowed in. The door was shut behind us.

Ruth wiped her forehead off with a dry towel. "Well, how's that for your first day?" she asked.

A trill traveled thru my whole body connecting all of my nerves, searching for a place to go to ground and finding none pushing me to the point of exhilaration. I had watched a woman give birth for the first time. What a blessing it was to see life enter the world. I knew from that moment on I wanted to be her apprentice and learn all I could about what I had just witnessed. Joseph shook his head and laughed at me.

"She's going to fit right in," he said.

From that moment on, Joseph and I talked every day. Ruth taught both of us things about life and nature. We learned about different herbs and their uses. When we weren't studying, we were talking and playing together. I became part of the family and loved them both. The work was hard and there were times when I would be called upon in the wee hours of the night. I loved every bit of it though. I knew without doubt or hesitation I was born to help bring life into the world.

A single spark, a dash of age, and the friendship we developed as children turned into the flames of love. Our village enjoyed celebrating and often did so without real reason or cause. Life itself was a celebration. We knew of the pestilence and took it as a sign from God above as a blessing because it had not reached us.

Joseph, shy and tender, walked up to me that night, "Would you like to walk with me?"

"Alone? T'would not be proper," I replied.

"Not alone, just around," he said.

We walked for hours, talking about life and what we both wanted. He had an easy way about him. Joseph's warm kind heart was the most beautiful I had ever know. It was love sent from above. His hand brushed across mine, sending a shiver up my spine. I tingled inside, something I had never known. I blushed without meaning to. An unconscious smile crossed my face. Joseph peered into my eyes. Longing passed through my soul, imprisoning me in a desire to be closer to him. He stepped closer, my heart raced. When I looked down towards the ground, Joseph touched the bottom of my chin-heat filled me with that single touch.

"I've always been able to speak to you about everything," he said.

"I know," I said.

"Well, then why am I so nervous about this when all we are doing is walking and talking," he said.

I didn't speak, but just gazed into his beautiful eyes. They had a slight tint of yellow in them I hadn't noticed before.

Just before we walked back towards the celebration, he turned to me, "May I call upon you tomorrow to go for a ride with the horses?" he asked.

"Yes," I said, my voice just above a whisper.

The beginning of our love affair had been prepared for our entire lives. In what prison of death does life often give such painful and violent memories for us to hold on to? The pain resides in not ever knowing what life would have been like with my sweet Joseph. Our children never existed and the sweet tenderness of his skin and mine never had a chance to touch from within.

The devil himself used the sword of God to yank him out of my life. There are nights when I can still feel Joseph's soft tender touch and taste his sweet breath as it mingled with mine just before our lips would meet. It was his gentle nature that drew me to him. There is nothing greater or more important than the heart when it's in love. Still, when I look around me now, it is nothing more than a shadow's thorn created from loss.

Shattering are the times when death lingers in the mind, reminding you of all the things you could have done or should have said. Always leaving you with unanswered questions. The mysteries of life, nothing more than a series of memories and queries wanting to be tapped into and answered during times of strife. Did he really love me, I know he did.

It just wasn't enough to change the path I chose in death.

The Unkindness of Ravens

I remember being elated with sheer excitement when they first arrived. I had never seen such a show of strength and glory in men. Each rode upon a black horse and wore black uniforms, shrouded in white capes with a red cross on them. The horses sounded like thunder from far away and shook the ground I stood on. Still I could feel my heart race with excitement when they approached. What glory they held for me. Little did I know they carried death in their sheaths along with their swords.

All the villagers gathered to the square when they arrived. It was their pomp and circumstance that made us curious. Why would we be so special to deserve such thought?

"Who speaks for this village?" The man in front said.

"I will speak for this village. What brings the Templar Knights to us?" Father Leon asked.

Father Leon was a meek man who saw the value in talking things through rather than violence. He was the most trusted man in the village and never once in all the times I knew him did he ever harm anyone.

"There are rumors of devil worship and witchcraft. That is why your village is unscathed by the pestilence," the man said.

His stance was solid upon the horse, like he had seen many battles while sitting on the beast. His piercing steel grey eyes held zero warmth. His hand rested on his sword. I didn't realize then, but now I know, he itched to let it taste blood again.

I watched while the man I had known and loved all my life, began to tremble. His face grew pale and his eyes looked towards the ground. Defeated by his fear of the reputation the men held, he shrunk to the ground, pleading.

"I can assure you there is nothing like that here," Father Leon cried.

My stomach wrenched in a combination of pity and a muddled sense of confused pride. I didn't understand why Father Leon would shrink to the ground like a rat pleading for his life. Without provocation, the man pulled his bloodstained sword from an ornate sheath and unhinged Father Leon's head from his shoulders. Blood oozed down the front of his tunic to the ground. His body froze where it stood and then went limp. Everyone ran screaming in all different directions. The shock of seeing the blood run out of our Father sent me lost in a nightmare—no longer of my own body. Instead, I was a stranger in a land of guilt

Joann H. Buchannan

where souls screamed out for mercy that was never received. I don't know who set the first fire in the village. I only remember the smell of it made me gag.

It was a rancid smell, like rotting meat, only more sour than most. I looked back and saw one of the Templar Knights take the body of Father Leon and toss it on a fire as if he were nothing more than a pile of pestilence needing to be eradicated. The villagers scurried like rats in a field set ablaze. The knights rode, swards in-hand, cutting down my people one by one. I watched in horror as one of the knight's swords sliced through little Tanner's body. A scream flew from my lips; I heard it before I realized it was mine.

Joseph rushed down from the hills. He looked right at me and stopped. Our eyes met. For one split second I thought hope had sent me a message. We were going to live.

A thunderous sound from behind the hill caused him to turn around. I yelled out to warn him but I was too late. I watched a man shove a sword through his chest. My soul went numb the moment the blade went through his body. The world stopped moving forward. His eyes locked on mine one last time. I must have screamed out again, because the man looked at me with a grin on his face then he mouthed the words, 'For God.'

I watched the man reach into Joseph's skull and pluck his beautiful eyes out.

I reached my arm out towards him. There was nothing I could do. A knight on a horse rushed up behind me. I screamed out in terror when I turned and met his blade. Somehow, he missed me. I don't know why.

"I am here to cleanse this village of its evil. I will start with all those who I see as witches. This is the will of God!" he yelled.

"Who's will is it that we all burn for a sin we did not commit?" I yelled out.

The same knight, who killed my Joseph, walked towards me. I felt more than hatred in his eyes when he looked upon me. Still frozen in shock, I stayed where I was. He grabbed my arm. Hatred welled up to the point of explosion. I prayed right then he would suffer more pain than all he had caused. With all my might I tried to shove him off me. A putrid smell exuded from his pours. His breath smelled like dried blood. For a second, I was sure he himself was the very demon he accused us of conjuring.

"You are a brave one? Aren'tcha witch?" he said to me.

I heard my name screamed out from a distance.

"Julia!"

I felt my heart drop, I knew that voice. It was my sister, Rowena. Tears streamed down her face. She stood frozen in her muddy blood soaked dress.

"Rowena!" I yelled out.

I tugged against the man who held my arm. I couldn't free myself from his shackled grip. He pushed me to the ground and raised his sword to my chin. I felt his other hand rip the skirt of my dress and reach for that which belonged to my now dead love. Pain thrashed between my legs. I knew I was no longer pure. I saw the unmistakable look of pleasure in the eyes of the man who took my life. He had satisfied himself inside me then slit my throat. Death did little to end my pain.

All at once I knew death contained both light and dark. Death, the eternal force that draws in all that is living, towards an inevitable fate. The universe does not make mistakes; nor does it waste a single ounce of energy. Death carries a strength and density all its own. Death is not to be tarried with nor given out so freely. We are all transformed into that from which we lived or died. I chose the latter. Death.

I watched as my sister's soul drifted towards the light. I couldn't do that. I wanted the men who stole our lives to pay for all they had done. They who had ripped love and beauty out of the world without reason needed to suffer.

A stale darkness surrounded my soul. In front of me hovered a being—one not of the living world. He had four faces. A lion, an eagle, a ram and the last was blank all accept the eyes. Long feathered wings of light and fire stretched out from its back. He wore an armor made of bronze. On its head rested a crown made of thorns and roses. Blood dripped down on the faces and the feet were laces with glittering wings.

"Become that which you couldn't in life," he said.

"Where am I?"

"In between."

He raised his arms, a flash from my village appeared. Smoke rose from the ground-it created a wall of black over the village. Fire raged against the death of the sun's gentle light, and all I had known was gone. The burned tattered ruins filled my heart with hatred.

"Use that," it said. "Make them pay."

My soul filled with anger. It exploded from me through the screams of many voices. Invisible, I walked around my burning village. I careened my body into the closest building I stood next to. Fire ate everything in sight like a starving wolf. On instinct, I put my arms up to guard me from the collapsing roof. Anger clutched onto the deepest reaches of my soul. I let out a shriek of many voices.

Darkness fell over the land, leaving behind the burned embers of a ruined village. The dwindling fires of the night had a golden hue. I could still smell the rancid burning flesh of those I loved. The ground was littered with the body parts. Not even the innocent children were spared. Having been Ruth's apprentice, I knew each of the faces of the children I looked at. Tiny Paul, who just had his second birthday, lay clutching his favorite blanket. His body, covered in blood. A single wound to his tiny chest was all it took to dispatch the little boy in front of me. I leaned over his body and tried to run my fingers through his hair. He loved his forehead rubbed when he was in pain. Perhaps this time it was an attempt to soothe my own pain. The hushed sound of the children's cries rang in my ears.

I wandered through the village and found my love...my Joseph. Where his eyes once rested, there were now only two bloody hollowed cavities. He was going to wander the afterlife blind. What sin had he committed to deserve such desecration?

I leaned over and touched my ghost-like lips upon his, praying to feel the warmth I had just hours before. Nothing. All that I once was now lost in a sea of anger and rage. I screamed so loud an unfamiliar shrill left my throat and stretched out amongst the living and the dead.

Joseph's body jumped. I screamed again. He sat up. Shock went through me like a second soul.

"Joseph? Are you still alive?" I whispered in his ear.

No breath came from his body. I felt his energy. I moved my head to the left. His followed. I stood. He came with me. We were two of the same yet I was the one with the strings and I loved the feel of his energy.

The grass beneath his body changed to the bright ember color of fire. It turned to ash. It shriveled and turned to cold stagnant dust and I didn't understand what happened or why Joseph's body moved or why the grass beneath us lit up and turned to ash.

I leaned in, placed my invisible arms around his chest and tried to hear his heartbeat. Again, nothing; and yet he was mobile on his own. I peered into the hollowness where his eyes once were.

One of the knights came up the hill from the village. "Aye, I got one of the demon bastards over here."

My body drifted from ethereal to solid for a moment and let out another shrill high pitched scream. Cracked grey flesh formed upon my body. What power had I found in death that I did not have in life? Why was I not able to stop them before they slaughtered my village and shattered my life? The answer really didn't matter at the time.

Like millions of red fireflies, the winds carried floating embers across the whole field. Beautiful and terrible as time itself, the scene that surrounded me was nothing more than energy lending itself to me to bend as I pleased. They, who brought death with them in the name of God, would now experience the terror they had inflicted on so many.

I screamed my banshee cries and moved. Joseph's body moved with mine. We were like dancers on a ghostly stage. I felt the coldness of the decaying corpse. I raised my arm and his body mimicked. A surprised thrill pulsated through my soul. I had a power unlike anything I had ever known or felt. Life's energy had been given to me to control. I still didn't understand the consequences of my actions. All I could see was a way to make the Templar Knights pay for what they had done.

"I will be your eyes tonight my love," I said.

Without sight, Joseph did as I commanded. He picked a blade up from the ground and walked towards the unwitting man that headed our way. From the darkness, Joseph laid death's blow into his neck. A single slice was all it took to force the man to his knees. That wasn't enough for me though. I wanted more.

What is it to want more? What drives a soul to need something so much it doesn't see the ruin and devastation it leaves in its wake?

The Templar Knight grabbed for his neck with both hands. Satisfied, I watched his soul leave his body. His eyes grew wide with fear when he looked into mine.

Joann H. Buchannan

"Know this. You will walk the land and haunt the very ground you cursed on the day you rode into this village," I said.

"You have no say in my soul demon! Only God has a say."

I scoffed in his face at his unwillingness to see that it was an innocent soul who had been wronged in life that was now judging his fate. I felt my voice grow deep and change from one to many.

"You were a twisted soul even in life. I am the messenger, and the word I carry is a curse upon you and all who rode with you." I told him.

Fate has such a way as to give you what you need the moment you need it. What most of us forget is that it always comes with a price. Pay as you go. Pay as you will. Either way, Fate will have her way and we will all do her bidding.

Anger swelled inside me again as the man, even in death, held fast to his twisted idea of what God wanted or needed.

32

"Witch! Demon. Devil's child. I will not tolerate this from—"

"I was not a witch or a demon. I was innocent of all you have claimed me to be. I was in love with a beautiful man. I had dreams of a family and you ripped that out from under me without even asking me what I believed! Be quiet!" I scoffed.

Deep from within the heart of my soul, I felt the rage boil to the surface again. Consequences or not, I now understood the power I wielded. I had become the sickle of death.

"Let's play a game, shall we?" I asked the now silenced man beside me.

A shrill sounded from my entire being. A funnel of burned ash enveloped us and more of the land hardened beneath us.

I watched the corpse of the man rise up. His severed neck could barely stand the weight of his head. The sound of squished blood and bones sent a thrill through my entire being. I knew what I wanted to do and I couldn't wait to watch what I had created.

I turned towards Joseph, "You are free. Pass on and remember how much I loved you," I said.

With that, Joseph's body fell to the ground once more. With the movements of a puppeteer, I danced with the body of the knight. The rest of the knights had created a campsite over the hill and towards the middle of the clearing. A burned ember, color of ash, surrounded us with each step we took. My hell approached against the moonless dark of the night. Where I was once afraid of the dark, I now felt at home being one of the unnatural.

"Robert, hurry up and get over here," one of the men yelled.

"So that's your name huh?" I said towards the soul who followed me in silence.

He grimaced. I smiled.

"Never thought a demon would know my name."

"NOT A DEMON!"

I raised my hand into the air. His motions mimicked mine. My sweet innocence was now gone. It was replaced by a phantasm of bloodlust and an overwhelming desire to see those who had destroyed life itself, suffer. Dead footsteps under my control walked towards the unsuspecting inhabitants of the camp.

I turned to Robert. Wrapped in chains, his shredded grey spirit stared back at me. I took my finger and raised it to my eyes. His hands mimicked my movement. With his decaying fingernail, Robert's body scratched at the hollow dead eyes left in his body.

"No, please don't leave me here blind as well," Robert's spirit pleaded.

"It was nothing less than what you did to Joseph," I replied.

I felt a grin cross my face as the dead fingers dug deeper into the sockets of the eyes. A small amount of fluid squirted out against the pressure. I had to laugh a little when I realized the popping sound often made by me as a child was the same sound his eyes made when they popped out of his skull. I took more pleasure in this than perhaps I should have. Still pleading with me, Robert screamed out when he could no longer see in the spirit world.

A glance to the right of the camp made pain's sting sharpen. I saw Rowena's body on the ground near the woods. Her face had been slit through the mouth. One of her fingers had been cut off. Her dress had been turned to nothing more than shredded cloth rags. I looked back at Robert's spirit.

"What did you do to her?" I asked.

"Who, oh the girl? She was given the opportunity to tell the truth about the village. She chose not to. Her torture took a while. I'm sure George took his time. It's his way," a smile formed across Robert's face.

Echoes of her screams rang through the darkness of my heart.

"Julia!"

She had tried to warn me. She wanted to protect me. Me. Me. ME! I was the one person who didn't look upon the men as if they were killers when they first arrived. I was the one who was taken in by the pomp and circumstance. I was the one who didn't seem to understand they were bad men. They were sent to kill us.

Hells fire and brimstone was in my grasp and could be given now to those who had wronged all of us. That was my focus. That was the curse I planned on laying at their feet. That was the curse I chose for myself. They made the demon they sought.

I heard the ooze with every step as Robert's body drew near the camp. None of the men looked up at him. I wanted them to though. I needed to see the look of fear in their eyes when they looked upon his already decaying body. I wanted the putrid smell of what I had created to inch its way into their nostrils. They needed to know death had come for them, just like they had brought it to so many unsuspecting people.

I let out a banshee cry in the night causing the horses to stir and the forest around us to silence. All of the men remained soundless and still. None of them looked up except to see the horses. I forced Robert's body to pick up the ax on the ground next to a log.

Step by cautious step, I walked the body towards the closest Templar Knight.

"Good, Robert's here. We can give thanks and eat," one of them said.

The man said eat. Eat. EAT! They slayed my village and were going to EAT.

It forced the rage inside me to grow louder. The surrounding trees burst into flames when I let out another rage-filled scream. More ash flew around us. I felt the trill of life's energy flow through my soul. One of the horses let out a pain-filled wince. Its body hardened and turned to stone. More ember ashes darted against the breeze. The rest of the horses jumped again. The men looked over at the trees and crossed their chests. Still they didn't see the Robert body I controlled.

With all the skill I could muster at the time, I balanced the body with the ax in hand. Even in my ethereal state, I felt the heavy rigidity of the dried blood-covered ax. If I had a heart, the pounding of it would have echoed like drums in the night. Wild and alive in my ghostly state, I moved the Robert body closer to the campsite.

"What's that smell?" one of the men said.

I hovered over them, waiting for that single moment when they looked towards Robert's body. The dangerous combination of fear and curiosity thickened the ember ash-filled air.

The leader stepped out of his tent. His gray eyes widened with shock. In an instant, he unsheathed his sword. It brought me back to the moment my world changed.

I moved across the clearing with grace and ease as I commanded the decaying Robert body.

"Bloody hell, what demon has taken one of our men?" the man said.

The men around the fire picked up their swords and swung away at the body. I raised my arm, to make the body swing the ax. In a single blow, I took out a knight. A screech came from the heart of my soul. The horses scattered at the sound emanating from within me. Corporeal skin cracked across my body. Nails grew from the tips of my fingers, sending a shooting pain through my being.

I now had two bodies under my control. My voice screamed out in many voices. I pulled the energy within me again. I knew the transfer now. The ground rumbled from beneath us. The leaves from the trees crackled and burned as the life force drained from within. Once again, my soul drifted from ethereal to solid. The fractures that had blanketed me before were no longer grey. Reborn to the night, the softness of life had come to caress me once more in death's cold embrace.

I felt the life energy around me flow into my spirit and out towards the lifeless bodies. With one hand I controlled Robert's body. With my other hand I now had another puppet at my disposal. I pulled more energy from wherever it came. High above the land, I looked down upon the knights who now ran towards the woods in terror.

More ash swirled about, landing on the tent the man appeared from. The tent burst into flames and landed on one of the knights. He raced off into the night. I watched his soul leave his body and took control of the burned corpse. The fire lit the ground around me. I saw the grey matter beneath the dead and still it didn't dawn on me as to why.

The knights raged against the new army of their slain fellow soldiers. Blood spilled from the already-decaying fighters. The oozing blood dripped on the fire sending out the putrid stench of death. The corpse of a man burned beyond all recognition, now raised his sword to do my bidding. Warmth came off the burned warrior. I could see part of his ribcage and his entire face was gone. I looked back at the soul of the man who had burned. Wires went through his eyes. On the top of his head was a hand with claws. The claws were dug into his skull. It pulsated like it was feeding on him. I let out a laugh. That which had been taken in life was now freely given in death.

"We cannot kill what is already dead!" one of the Templar Knights yelled.

"Stand your ground! Do not let the demon hold the bodies of our fallen," the leader yelled.

"In the name of God, how do we defeat this evil?" another asked.

I heard heavy breath from within the darkness. The men stilled themselves. Their beating hearts pulsated through the air. I waited. I knew they were praying to the same god I had prayed to all my life. Yet here I was, an innocent turned towards the dark because of their actions. Why couldn't they have asked us what we felt to be good and honest and true?

What in the darkness could be worse than that of the imagination of an innocent soul that had been wronged? There was little left to guess. The men knew they were going to die. I could hear it in the beating of their hearts. The faster they beat the more I knew the fear of what I had become struck closer to the depths of their souls. This caused so much doubt in what they had become in life.

Murderers.

Templar Knights.

Men of God!

I became an army of the dead. The men stabbed my fighters to no avail. They rushed the bodies, tackling them to the ground. I laughed at the once proud strong men and their great might that were now reduced to nothing more than the annoyance of a mosquito bite. The sound of crushed bones shuddered through me with an orgasmic thrill. With a swing of the ax in Robert's hand, I cut off the hand of one of the men. A scream of pain filled the ever growing silence of the wild.

From behind me I felt the two souls of the men making their way towards me. I turned and faced them. They held the same look of hatred in death as they had in life. The sheer force of evil in them erupted through. One of the men let out a shrill. His face had been contorted. An extra mouth formed on his cheek. Wire wrapped him from his hands to his ankles. A hand floated over him with a knife in it. It sliced parts of his soul off and fed it to the extra mouth.

"A pound of flesh for each life you took," I said.

The other soul knelt down to the ground. I smelled the youth of his soul. Such a shame. I watched hell unleash such wrath on the young soul. It sucked his soul into the night. From the darkness I heard tiny mouths chew on his essence. He begged for God's forgiveness.

"Please, we didn't know. We thought we were doing the work of God," the newly dead man pleaded.

A smile formed across my face. I let out the screech of multiple voices in the night reaching both animal and man. I turned my focus back to the fight. A single blow to the head of one of the charging men landed him on the ground. Pieces of his brain dripped onto his face. Half his skull gone, once again I let out the scream deep from within. I felt the power of the world beneath my feet.

Hell's gates opened and I was able to see what atrocities he had committed. His soul stood upon a pillar in the darkness. A spear sliced through the top of his head and down the center. It exited through his crotch. His soul dangled on the spear while fireballs were flung at him. The gates closed. The thorn of revenge filled me with a sweet satisfaction.

Those who I chased called out against the evil I had done. Evil, they said. As if they were innocent to all they had chosen to do. If I had blood, it would have boiled. Instead I turned back toward the other dimension of the earth. The tactile of the ground beneath me had changed. No longer soft and smooth, it was now cold, hard stone.

Ash lit the night like a million red fireflies. They swirled around me in a gust of wind as invisible as me. In a flash of bright amber color, they lit the night up around me. For a just a moment, I wasn't invisible. They turned to ash and drifted towards the ground like a blast of beautiful black haunting feathers of death.

The devil blues had raped the land of life and given me power over it. With intention, I walked towards the forest the knights had scattered into like flies. The spell brought to me by the angel of death was like a drug, and I wanted more.

"Shhhh," I said. The echoing sound bounced off the trees.

A panicked drum sound of a heartbeat inched its way towards me. I moved my puppets towards the sound. Their oozing bodies, limp and unsavory looking—had slow, steady steps. I felt a new hunger grow inside me. A need to taste the very essence of their souls grew like a fire within my belly. With an animalistic nature I sped towards the drums of the beating heart.

Flesh upon soul upon flesh, I entered one of the rotting corpses just to find out if I could. To my surprise, the ooze of the body fit what I had become. The men, knights of honor and goodness were the unkindness of ravens set upon my village with little regard for life. And I—oh how I now had little regard for their souls. With

Joann H. Buchannan

the borrowed flesh, I slashed through the brush to reach the ever faster beating heart. The knight, a young man with fresh eyes looked up at me and screamed out in terror and backed himself into a large tree.

Everything around me continued to clash with the invisible wind and burn. The amber ash landed on the knight. Each piece that touched his skin burned brighter. The face of the knight turned gray and hardened. His sculpted stone body bared the mark of fear and I was the artist of the masterpiece. The force of my wrath was so strong it carried through him and to the tree he laid against. His arm, frozen in time, was held up to guard his face like a vampire hiding from the light of day.

Multiple voices in dark laughter leaped from my throat when I let out a howling. Menacing as it was, it didn't compare to the pain the knights had put us through.

The Eternal Choice

The dead began to outnumber the living. Like a shadow and thorn, the memories of the people I loved flashed through my mind. In life, I helped new life enter the world. In death, I took those to my side of the multiverse. Angel, vixen, demons and gods — all had a price and I gladly paid.

The last of the clearing crackled and turned to dust and stone. From off in the distance I heard a familiar voice call my name. A shock of electricity filled my being. Could it be? My dear sweet Joseph was here for me.

"Julia."

I rushed into his arms. No longer did he feel lifeless and cold. Our mouths a breath apart—he leaned in and kissed me. I filled with passion as Joseph ran his hands through my hair. His lips lingered at my neck, causing us to be lifted up as if on the wind like seed of cotton with exhalation and excitement. The love we had known in life had carried over into death. I didn't want to lose him again. Holding onto me, he looked at me with his hollowed eyes. I didn't shun or shy away. I knew he was the same beautiful soul I had known in life.

"I won't leave without you," he said.

"It's already too late. We were robbed of our lives. Our futures."

"We still have eternity," he said, his lips brushed mine.

Our invisible bodies intertwined and we floated up towards the sky. A bright light shined above us.

"You have to go, before it's too late," I said to him.

"Even God would forgive such a vengeance. He made all things. Even the power you possess now," he said. "I will not leave without you."

"Listen to the boy, witch," Robert's soul shouted out.

"You have no say here!" I said.

I felt my anger waver against the darkness my soul was becoming. I would have taken Joseph's hand if I hadn't heard the Templar Knights whispering in the darkness. It was as if the trees carried their words to my ears.

"I knew I was right when I slayed the priest. Look at the demon they have unleashed here."

It was the leader. The look of fear in his eyes, the final beheading of the priest who baptized me hitting the ground, screams from my sister and last but not least, Joseph; dear sweet Joseph who was as God fearing as the land itself. I knew then I could not stop until they all paid.

"I have more sorrow than you will ever know, but God created all things, even the wickedest for His day of reckoning," I told him.

I turned away from Joseph and forced the dead to do more of my bidding. It was time for all of it to end.

With the night comes the power of the universe. It is merciless and doesn't worry about what the next day brings. I didn't know what was happening to the world around me. All I knew was the night was far from over and I had to complete what I had started. The devil of vengeance stood at my side and I took his hand in mine, for now he was my love and I became what the rest in my village could not. I became Death.

My control grew with each passing moment. I now outnumbered what was left of the knights. I forced the rotting corpses into the depths of the forest. Their broken bones clicked with each step. They marched to do my bidding leaving behind a trail of blood and abandoned limbs. Some could wield swords, others continued with only torsos the pieces of them still whole enough to fight, to bite or scratch at the foes they tracked.

I walked them through the forest in an unwavering approach of the final remaining knights. I knew who I was saving for last. I knew it before the night's terror began. The leader would cower to me and what I had become because of him.

Two men were crouched down in the brush of the forest. They held their breath so as not to make a sound. I followed the stench of fear and fast beat of their black hearts. The bodies, my bodies, crushed every one of them. The two men fought back with no hope for escape. I watched while one by one they were crushed. The sound of their breaking bones echoed through the forest. It was music to my soul.

Bloodied and battered, one by one they became mine to control. We came upon the last man standing. I wanted more than anything for the man to see me and know who had delivered death through the night to meet him face to face.

With every ounce of my strength, I screamed at the top of my lungs. I felt my soul once again charge up with power. I hovered above my puppets and looked down upon the leader's head. His fingers would be mine for pleasure. I knew I wanted him to suffer the most. Without his actions, my village would still be alive. I would still be getting married soon and laughing with my sister. My life would still exist.

My puppets circled the leader of the Templar Knights. He cowered in fear and prayed to whatever God he believed in. His body trembled. His brow covered in sweat. I had Robert's body grab him from behind. The half-skull man took his sword and brought it down on the knight's fingers, severing them. They lay on the forest floor. The man screamed in pain. I laughed at the sight of the once strong man. I reached out with the mouths of my puppets and began to rip the flesh from his body. Blood spilled to the ground that was now hardened to stone.

I had another one of the bodies pick his fingers up from the ground and had it dig at the leader's eyes. He screamed out in pain once again. The souls of the men I had taken winced at the pain I forced on the leader.

"Just take my life, demon. You will never get my soul," he cried.

I smiled down on him. Once again I let out a scream and felt my body power up. With the last ounce of power I had. I made the dead that were mine rip the man apart. His body pieces lay on the bloodied ground. There was nothing left for me to do. I looked back at the men whose souls were under my control.

"You should have never come to my village seeking evil, George," I said.

"You're a demon. We came to kill you," the leader said.

"I was not a demon until you made me what I am tonight," I replied. "We were innocent of all you had accused us of. We were God fearing people with good hearts."

"How do you explain tonight then deceiver?"

"You sought evil. You brought death. It was given back in return," I said.

The souls of the dead were mine to do with as I pleased. I had no use for them and knew fire and brimstone awaited—especially for the leader. I saw what he did to my sister; he would feel the torture he thrust upon her. With every slice, intrusion of her body and smell he had given her. He would feel it tenfold. I watched something take him from behind. It forced itself on him with a great amount of enthusiasm. It then took a bite from his ear. George was forced to endure all the pain he had inflicted on so many. He would get to enjoy it for all eternity.

As dawn approached, I thought for a moment I might be able to still have that eternity with Joseph, but the light of day often brings about the consequences of the night. I looked around to see the ground was no longer full of life. Everything had hardened to stone, petrified. I had stolen my power from the life that existed all around me. I had taken more than just the lives of the Templar Knights. I had taken life itself. There would be no happy ending for me, of that I was sure.

Without warning, darkness surrounded me again. The angel with the four heads landed next to me. He put his arm around my shoulders.

"You have done well," he said.

"I have become what I feared the most," I replied.

"They were the evil scourge of the land. They needed purged and you were brave enough to do it," he replied.

"Who are you?"

"Malach HaMavet, the angel of death and light," he said.

The four-headed being looked down upon me with the blank face.

"I wish to mimic your face," he said.

"What would the angel of death need with my face?"

"As you see, I have a blank. I have waited thousands of years to find the right one,"

"What happens to me?" I asked.

"You will be with me."

I knew the being had a power stronger than mine, but I couldn't be what he wanted me to be. I gulped, as if I still had a body.

"I want to be with Joseph," I said. "Can you make that happen?"

"I can," he said.

I felt my soul meld into the body of the four headed angel. The blank on his fourth side, now replaced by my own face. The power of the universe opened up before me. Once again, it came with a price. The gates of heaven opened. Joseph stepped out through the blinding light.

"I'm not leaving without you," he said.

"No, this isn't right, I thought you said I could go with him," I said to the angel.

"I said you could be with him," he said.

"Joseph, I can't let you sacrifice your immortal soul to be with me," I cried.

Tears streamed down my face, reminding me that spirits could cry.

"I won't leave without you," Joseph said.

He wrapped his arms around me and held me while I cried.

"This isn't your choice to make," he said.

"It's what I asked for," I told him.

"No, you asked to be with me, I chose to come here to be with you," he said.

His lips brushed mine. Soft and tender as the first time we kissed.

"Besides, what is eternity without you?"

We roamed the forest, making love under the stars and talking for hours. We had a past, and in a way — a future. The one thing I wanted was the love of my life. I wanted to feel him for all eternity and I received my wish. Although it wasn't in a way I expected. Still, he was with me. We often came upon children who were lost in the woods. They each died of one thing or another. Together we assist them in the crossing over.

It is the dark side of my soul I fear the most. Malach HaMavet had my face, so for thousands of years we have roamed the stone trees of my creation. I brought death to those who sought it. I'm no longer the innocent child I was in life. I am the immortal revenant. I am the soulless light.

About the Author

Joann H. Buchanan, author, radio show host and mother of 5, is living in Kansas. Soulless Light is her debut piece. She is currently working on Night Walkers, book 1 of The Burning Times series.

She hosts The Eclectic Artist Cave Mon-Fri on The Shark at 11 AM CST. She interviews writers, producers, musicians and creative people of all kinds. Information about her show can be found at, http://theeclecticartistcave.blogspot.com.

She is currently represented by agent Chamein Canton who is pitching her young adult novel, I AM WOLF to publishers.

Some of her work can also be found on Scribd.com and her short story blog, http://joannhamann.blogspot.com.

She lives by two mottos, above all else, entertain and make it work.